# Wickedly Sweet

Steph Macca

# Contents

# Stalk the Author! Pretty Please.

**Readers Group**

**Steph Macca's Asylum for Pectoral Perves**

https://www.facebook.com/groups/authorstephmacca

**Instagram**

https://www.instagram.com/authorstephmacca/

**TikTok**

https://www.tiktok.com/@authorstephmacca

**Facebook**

www.facebook.com/authorstephmacca/

# Website

www.stephmacca.com

# Trigger Warnings and Foreword

Trick or treat... give us something *Wickedly Sweet* to eat.

This book contains some triggers which may be a turn off to some. These include primal play, CNC, blood/knife play, stalking/chasing, BSDM, including bondage, masturbation (surely not, but you never know!), choking, and general dirty roughness.

It's also important to note a few things:

- I have sadly never been to Salem or New York (Yet! Both are on my bucket list), so all information is to the best of my research and knowledge. Any inaccuracies should be taken with a grain of salt and enjoyed as fiction.

- I'm also a full-blooded, swearing Aussie, so some language and descriptions may not be accurate or entirely correct. Once again, with a grain of salt and spanks, thanks.

- The female main character is an inexperienced virgin... but hey, that doesn't mean she doesn't have a dirty, dark side. After all, we all do. That's why you've picked up this book, isn't it?

- This book is just a novella, which means unfortunately it's short and sweet (just as long as the peens aren't) and as such, previous character development and build up is limited. Enjoy it for what it is and as it comes... (wink wink)

Happy Halloween!

*To all my bad bitches who live vicariously through smut books.*

*This one is for you.*

*Because while we wouldn't necessarily want to be fucked with a knife, we sure as shit want to read about it.*

# Chapter 1

---

*Ahh... Salem, Massachusetts.*

There was something about this city that spoke to my little black heart. I'm not sure if it's the slightly chilled weather, the old buildings, or the presence of ghosts, but whatever the reason, it feels like home.

It would also hopefully be the nice, needed distraction from my recent misery.

"Audrey, are you even listening?"

I pull my Airpods out of my ears and look at my brother, Tyler, in the driver's seat. "Huh? Did you say something?"

He sighs, rolling his eyes while glaring at me through the rear-view mirror.

"I asked if you wanted anything from the gas station shortly."

"Oh," I mutter, starting to put an Airpod back in. "No, I'm good."

Tyler mutters under his breath, looking at his friend Brax in the passenger seat.

"I can't believe my parents made me bring her with us."

I stare daggers at him. "I can still hear you, asswipe."

The car falls silent except for quiet chuckles from the other two passengers. We are on our way to Salem for Halloween, a much needed trip for me. But Tyler is annoyed that he had to bring his baby sister with him and his two friends for the annual witch hunt and Halloween festivities.

The three of them are 20, only two years older than me, so it's not like it's a case of dragging a *child* with them. But to Tyler, it's an annoyance that he tried to fight our parents on. Thankfully, Mom sided with me and agreed to let me go on their trip. After all, our parents are funding it.

"I don't understand why you had to tag along on our boys' trip. You could have stayed at home and read your lame books or something."

Tyler's brown eyes narrow on me, and I'm temporarily concerned that he will crash the damn car if he doesn't look at the road.

"Well, too bad. It's not like I plan to spend all my time with you three. I just want to do my own thing and enjoy myself."

It's true. I have no intention of hanging out with the three of them much. I just needed to get out of New York. Or rather, I need to get away from someone.

"It's no wonder Josh broke up with you. Probably stuck to him like a damn leech too."

The reminder of my ex-boyfriend sends a wave of anger down my spine. Everyone seems to have it in their heads that Josh dumped *me.* But in reality, I dumped *him.*

Despite the fact I had spent the last two years thinking he could be the one, it was an easy decision.

Especially when I found him balls deep inside his new female best friend. You know, the one he told me not to worry about.

It's a sensitive topic. The fucker tried to gaslight me, telling me he has *needs*. Apparently, respecting my body and decisions was not an option. But little did Josh know, I had actually planned to give him my virginity next week on his birthday.

Oh, well. Bullet dodged, I guess.

A voice rumbles from beside me in the back. "Cut her some slack, T. She's good."

I look over at Nate, giving him a small thank you smile. Nate nods, his tanned skin, blue eyes, and brown hair sending murderous butterflies into my stomach.

*Gotta kill those butterflies. All men are off limits right now.*

Brax laughs, shoving Tyler gently in the arm. "I don't think your sis will cockblock you. Besides, we don't mind if she tags along."

Tyler grumbles, eyes finally back on the road. "She's annoying though."

"What's annoying is hearing about your plans to bang it out. I'm not going to be tied to you while you try to pick up sexy Harley Quinns and kittens, so calm down, Fabio."

The car erupts into sniggers as Tyler's cheeks redden. He turns into the gas station a little too sharply, making me slide into the door.

"Ow! Seriously?" I ask, rubbing my elbow.

"I'll be back," snaps Tyler, getting out of the car and slamming the door.

I shake my head, tapping my phone to change songs. Happier Than Ever by Billie Eilish starts playing as I reach to put my second Airpod in.

"Don't worry about him," Brax says, unclicking his seat belt. "He's just moody because the chick he was into turned him down. We're fine with you coming."

Brax's green eyes find mine before switching to Nate's. His soft, curled blonde hair looks almost see-through as the sunlight streams through the car.

Nate nods, stretching his arms. "And for the record, T is more into sexy nurses. Though I don't think he'd turn down a Harley Quinn."

I snort, tilting my head back. "Yeah, well he's a Joker, that's for sure."

We pull up at the Salem Inn, a quaint building with red bricks. Tyler had ignored me for the rest of the drive, and I happily zoned out, listening to music. My phone had been blowing up with messages from Josh, but I left them unread, not interested in whatever it is he has to say.

As far as I'm concerned, he no longer exists in my world, and he is free to put his dick in a blender.

"Welcome!" the innkeeper says with a big grin as we enter. His aging face is nothing but polite and warm as he glances between the four of us. I return a smile, hovering back from the guys as they approach the check-in desk. Tyler pulls a piece of folded paper from his wallet, sliding it to the innkeeper.

"We have four rooms booked. Here's the reservation confirmation, if it helps."

The innkeeper scans the paper, nodding. "Perfect. I've got keys for you all. If you need anything during your stay, just come down and see me. I'm Alex, and I'm here most of the time."

I note a brochure stand and I walk over, my eyes taking in the information on local attractions. We are only here for three days, but I want to do as much as I can before I have to return to reality. Alex looks over at me, pointing to the bottom row.

"There's some great little restaurants there. If you're looking for things to do, there's heaps of Halloween events on."

I grab a few brochures to read in my room. "That's great to hear. I'm really excited to check out the town."

Alex hands over four sets of keys to Tyler, his salt and pepper hair sticking up at odd angles. "Do you have anything in mind yet?"

Tyler hands out the keys, dumping mine in my awaiting open palm. I fiddle with them, the cold metal warming up from my touch.

"I want to do the witch hunt. It's in two days, right?"

He grins, nodding. "Yes. On Halloween. Are you going to be a witch or a hunter?"

"Definitely a witch," I laugh.

The three guys look at me with mixed expressions. Tyler looks like he is sucking on a sour lemon, while Nate and Brax give me an intrigued, questioning glance.

"Are you boys going to do it too?" asks Alex.

"Hell, no," answers Tyler, tossing his key in the air and catching it. "I have better things to do than play silly little games."

I roll my eyes, sending Alex an apologetic smile. "He's as fun as a wet blanket."

"To each their own," smiles Alex. "I'm sure you will all find something enjoyable to do. That's the allure of Salem... anyone can find a little magic."

My room is beautiful. The antique vibes make me feel like I'm back in the 1600's, but with a touch of modern decor. The room is cozy and surprisingly warm for fall.

I place my bag on the double bed, unzipping it to pull out some clothes. It's nearly dinner time, and I reluctantly agreed to eat with the guys. Well, Nate and Brax offered. Tyler said nothing, but he's made his displeasure very known.

Tomorrow, I plan to explore the town on my own. I'm not sure what Tyler has planned, but I'm sure it involves searching for sex on legs.

I decide to take a quick shower before dinner to freshen up. I tie my dark cherry-red hair up in a bun to avoid it getting wet, and scrub myself with my mango exfoliating soap. When I finish, I wrap a towel around me, pulling out my make-up case. I'm not huge on make-up, but I do like it. I mostly just do my eyes as I can't contour to save my life.

Using my liquid eyeliner, I give myself a winged look, highlighting my blue eyes with some complimentary silver eyeshadow. Here, the extent of my make-up skills ends, so I complete the look with mascara and a clear lip gloss.

The weather outside is a little chilly, so I opt for a pair of torn black jeans, a red tank top and a grey hoodie. I don't bother to fix up my hair. I might not be a mom, but I sure as hell can rock a mom-bun.

By the time I step outside the inn, the guys are already waiting for me. Tyler is on his phone, his fingers vigorously swiping through matches on Tinder. I guess romance is dead, but then again, he probably doesn't know how to seduce a woman the old-fashioned way. Everyone is so impatient these days, relying on technology to do the heavy lifting.

"You look nice," comments Brax as I approach. I give him a warm smile, noting the three of them are dressed similarly to me, with jeans and hoodies.

"Thanks," I say, looking to Tyler. "Where do you want to go?"

Tyler shrugs, not looking up from his phone. "There's a NY-style pizza place nearby."

I roll my eyes. "Really? We didn't leave New York just to eat food from back home. Come on, it's nearly Halloween. I bet there are some great restaurants doing spooky shit."

Tyler sighs, locking his phone screen. "I don't really care for *spooky shit*."

"Then why did you even bother to come to Salem?"

He doesn't respond, shoving his phone into his hoodie pocket. Tyler looks at Nate, shrugging. "Any ideas?"

Nate looks up and down the street before motioning towards an intersection. "If you want pizza, why don't we go to Salem House of Pizza. We can walk past the cemetery too on the way back. Or even head towards the water and see the Haunted Witch Village."

Tyler pales but nods. Ha. He's a scaredy cat.

I remember a few years ago we were watching The Conjuring and he high-pitched screamed, trying to say it was a pinched nerve in his back. He promptly left the room for the remainder of the night, claiming he needed to rest.

I guess that's why they say siblings can be different. Because whereas Tyler is a chicken, I love horror. There's something about the thrill of being scared, the adrenaline that makes your heart pound while you fight your mind to stay in control. Then, once it's all over, the feeling of safety calms you... and you're so keen to feel the rush again.

Maybe I'm sick and twisted. But, there's a reason villains are often painted as hot, seductive men.

It's because women like me exist.

And we want to scream in more ways than one.

# Chapter 2

Dinner is amazing. Delicious, hot slices of pizza and wickedly sweet calzones for dessert. By the time we're finished, my body is happily buzzing from the tasty treats, but as soon as Brax mutters a trip to the Haunted Witch Village, Tyler suspiciously declares he has an impending case of food poisoning.

Nate, Brax and I share a look. We all know he's faking to get out of spooky horror, but we decide to play along. Nate, like a champion, volunteers to escort Tyler back to the inn.

"You don't have to come with me," I say sympathetically to Brax.

He grins and tucks a loose blonde curl behind his ear. "And leave you alone in an unfamiliar city? Nah. It will be fun. Besides, I want to go."

I watch the backs of Tyler and Nate as they walk off, before turning and heading the opposite direction with Brax.

"Thank you," I mutter finally, grateful that at least one male on this trip isn't an asswipe.

Brax looks at me, his eyes alight with amusement. "It's fine. Despite what T thinks, you're not bad company. In fact, it's nice to have someone who likes scary shit as much as me."

Laughing, I tuck my hands into my hoodie pockets. "Likewise. Tyler hates it even if he won't admit it, and Mom and Dad are more comedy fans. Halloween just calls to me in a way that the other holidays don't."

Brax nods, weaving us in and out of the passing crowd of people. "I'm lucky. My sister is into it too. But she's off at college now, so it's just me watching the scary movies back home."

"I'll come watch them with you," I offer politely, scowling as someone accidentally shoves me in the shoulder as they pass.

"That would be nice, as long as you're comfortable with it."

I snort, earning myself a surprised look from Brax.

"What?" he asks with a laugh.

"I've known you most of my life. I'm fairly certain you're not a serial killer."

Tyler has been friends with Nate and Brax since they started middle school. I practically grew up with them in the house. They visit often, especially in the summers where the three of them spend time around our pool. The only exception for me was last summer, when I had gone on a little trip with Josh.

The reminder of better times is a bitter pill to swallow, my face reflecting my thoughts.

Brax stops walking, making me halt. I look at him, my face twisting in surprise.

"What?" I ask, curiously.

He pulls us out of the way of oncoming walkers into a small alleyway. "You've been weird the past few days. Is this about your boyfriend?"

"*Ex*-boyfriend," I correct him, folding my arms. "And it's fine. I just get annoyed whenever he pops into my head."

Brax nods thoughtfully. "So, what happened?"

I rub my arm in slight discomfort, unsure how much information I want to share with my brother's best friend. "I dumped him. We had different interests."

"Different interests?"

I clear my throat. "Yes, well... I wanted to wait to have sex. And he didn't. Which unfortunately resulted in his dick falling into someone. Total accident, of course," I mutter sarcastically.

Brax raises an eyebrow, his face a mask of surprise and shock. "His loss then. You made the right choice."

"I know I did. But he keeps calling me and I don't have the patience to deal with him."

As if on cue, my phone buzzes again in my pocket. I sigh, reaching in to grab it. We both stare at the name on the screen, my finger poised over the button to reject the call.

I gasp as Brax snatches the phone out of my hand, sliding his finger across the screen to answer the call.

"What?" he snaps into the phone, his eyes ablaze with playful trouble.

His eyebrows crease slightly as he listens to whatever nonsense Josh is spouting down the phone, before humming thoughtfully.

"Right. Well, sorry asshole, but Audrey is a bit busy at the moment. We're both *busy*," he says suggestively.

I hear Josh yelling but, I can't make out the words. Brax grins at me, giving me a playful wink.

"I see. Well, I'll be sure to pass on the message when I've finished pounding her and making her scream my name until her throat is hoarse. Bye now."

He hangs up the phone, handing it back over to me. My body is shaking with silent laughter, though my cheeks are flaming red. I quickly turn my phone off, fully aware that Josh will try to call back.

"You're trouble," I laugh, putting my phone back into my pocket.

"Am I?" Brax responds innocently. "Or am I just the devil in disguise?"

I can't help but feel those damn butterflies again. I've never had someone stick up for me like that. Even if it was in a dirty, promiscuous way.

I guess the truth is that as much as I want to wait to have sex, I'm still as horny as every other 18-year-old. I think deep down, I knew that Josh wasn't the right one for me and he didn't deserve to have parts of me that should be sacred.

Brax looks across the street, his eyes lighting up. I follow his line of vision and snort when I find what he's looking at.

"Oh, come on. No," I say, though it's clear that I'm not really against it.

"It will be fun. Hell, maybe you can even send him some pictures. Accidentally, of course."

I bite my bottom lip, wondering if I'm crossing blurred lines. The flashing red neon lights on the shop front are almost the same as a red flag, and I have the unmistakable urge to run at it.

I've never stepped inside an adult toy shop before, but I have always wanted to. A few months ago, some friends and I had laughed about it, but being the baby of the group, I was still 17 and they didn't want to leave me behind, so we skipped it. Unfortunately, life has been so busy that we haven't had the chance to do it yet.

*Fuck it.*

We only live once, right?

"Alright, let's go," I grin, laughing as Brax lets out a little cheer of victory.

We cross the street when it's clear of cars. Brax gestures for me to go first.

"Ladies first."

"What a gentleman," I taunt, pushing the heavy door open.

Brax follows me inside, his voice lowering so only I can hear. "Ladies always go first, in every sense."

I bite down on my tongue, ignoring the innuendo in his tone. Truthfully, I've always had a little crush on Brax. And Nate too. But, I always ignored the feelings because Tyler would lose his shit. Besides, I see them so often around the house, the last thing I want to do is make things awkward.

Though... that's now debatable by our impromptu sex shop visit.

The shop is well lit, despite appearing dark on the outside. I'm not sure why, but I always assumed that adult shops would be dark and dingy, full of old perverts jerking off in the corners.

As I take in the layout, I realize that the shop is set up by sections. Along the wall to my left is a collection of movies. The wall to my right is bondage equipment, shelves full of rope, chains, handcuffs, ball gags, and tape. In the far corner, there is a rack of lacy, see-through costumes. And in the middle of the shop are stands filled with various sex toys. My cheeks heat up as I look at the nearest item... a vibrating butt plug.

"Holy fuck," I mutter under my breath, walking slowly through the shop. Brax is over by the bondage collection, his hands gently feeling different types of rope.

My feet stop as I come to the dildos, my interest peaking. I'm not completely innocent, but I never realized just how many colors vibrators had.

I lean closer to the shelf, looking at a purple realistic vibrator. They even have veins...

I reach out curiously, my fingers touching the box as I read the writing.

"That looks interesting," Brax's voice says from beside me.

Jumping, I pull my hand back quickly. Embarrassment seeps through my body, even more so when I spot a bundle of red rope in his hand.

"I'm just looking," I blurt out hastily.

Brax smirks at me before turning to the vibrator. "Well, it has seven different settings. I'd say that's pretty good."

"Is it?" I ask, refusing to look at him.

He lifts the box off the shelf, turning it to read the writing on the back. "Battery operated, water-proof, and easy to clean."

I'm lost for words when a husky, female voice grabs my attention.

"Do you folks need any help?"

I look over to find a petite, young woman with pink hair watching us. She can't be more than a few years older than me, but she oozes confidence and sexuality. I'm envious of that and wish I could be as open as she is when in the presence of buzzing dicks.

"We're just browsing," Brax answers politely. "Do you have any recommendations?"

The woman looks at us both with interest, trying to gauge our personalities. It's probably easy to tell that I'm inexperienced since I'm redder than the neon sign out front.

"Sure. Right this way," she says, motioning for us to follow.

Brax gives me a grin before following. I quickly take after them, my feet nearly stumbling as I struggle to stay poised.

The woman stops in front of another shelf. "Here's some great items for couples. It depends what you guys like, but there's lots of his and her options."

Brax nods while I quickly blurt out the words faster than a bullet.

"We're not a couple."

I feel bad, worried that I've made her feel awkward. But, she merely nods without a hint of discomfort.

"Well, in that case, I can show you some items individually. What do you like?"

Even without looking, I can feel Brax's eyes on me. They are both waiting for me to respond, and it's at this moment that I start wishing the floor would open up and swallow me.

"Uh, I don't know," I murmur quietly. "I've never had any ... things."

The woman's lips crack a small smile, realizing my *situation*. "Okay, well girl to girl, let me show you a few things."

Her brown eyes scan over items, before she grabs a few toys.

"Everyone is different, but most popular items for beginners are toys like clitoral vibrators or animal vibrators for internal penetration."

Beginners... like a video game where you advance levels. Except, I guess I'm still in training mode.

"Animals?" I ask with horror.

Both the woman and Brax laugh, making my stomach twist.

"Not like that," she says, handing me a box. "This is a rabbit vibrator. The little ears are prongs and the shaft has tiny balls to also give more pleasure."

I stare in disbelief at the pink vibrator, almost traumatized by the *ears* that would tickle my bits.

"Or, there's also a butterfly one."

Oh, God. Not the *butterflies* again.

I quickly grab the rabbit, holding it against my chest tight. "I'll just get this one."

The woman nods, looking at Brax. "Is there anything I can help you with?"

Brax holds the rope up. "I'm set. Though, if you have any more duct tape out back, I'd like to have a look. The only one left on the shelf is a bit too flimsy for me."

"Of course, I'll be right back," she says, heading towards a door behind the counter.

The air shifts as Brax and I wait alone. I try to think of something to say, but my mind is drawing blanks.

"So... duct tape? You can get that from the hardware store."

I realize instantly that I'm an idiot. Brax, however, just laughs.

"It's not that kind of duct tape, Aud. Different *purposes.*"

I snap my mouth shut, nodding once. Instantly, my mind is filled with images of being tied up and gagged with duct tape. You would think, for a virgin, the thought would horrify me. But instead, the warmth spills over from my cheeks, heading south. My body tenses as I feel myself getting wet. This is wrong on so many levels, yet

I'm drawn to the idea. Imagining someone taking away my control and strength is a kink I didn't know existed in my little innocent brain.

I must be messed up. Or broken.

Because all I can picture now is Brax tying my hands together while he gives me a dimpled smile.

# Chapter 3

We never did make it to the Haunted Witch Village.

The thought of carrying Bugs around scared the crap out of me more than any horror film.

Bugs... my new rabbit vibrator.

Even though he was in a discreet black plastic bag, I suddenly had the fear that people would be able to see through it and discover all my deep, dark, dirty secrets.

When I got back to the inn last night, I put it on the end of my bed and spent much of the night staring at it. My dreams were strange, blurry visions of me walking through a field, jumping as florescent pink rabbits and butterflies jumped out at me, buzzing.

I skip breakfast, texting Tyler to tell him I had plans to explore the town. He responds with a thumbs up emoji and I hide out in my room for as long as possible, making sure the coast is clear for when I do leave.

I need to get my costume for tomorrow's witch hunt. But, if anything, I'm also excited to explore Salem.

It looks like it will be a nice day. The sun is out, but there's a slight fall breeze. Auburn leaves are scattering the pathway, so I decide to pull out some boots.

As I start to get ready, I spot Bugs again. He's just daring me to let loose. Half my mind is filled with embarrassment, but the other half... the hormonal part, wants to give it a go.

I sit on the bed, staring at him.

"Okay, Bugs. It's just you and me here. I think we could be good friends, but I have trust issues. We need to take this slow."

Perhaps the Salem Inn is haunted and I'm being possessed. It's really the only possible explanation for why the fuck I'm talking to a vibrator.

Sighing, I bury my face in my hands. I don't know why I'm so shy. It's not like I don't masturbate. Everyone does. Hell, I've even watched porn many times. But this is the next big step in my sexuality.

"Just do it, you coward," I mutter to myself, reaching for the box. My fingers graze the sides as I lift it, bringing it into my lap. I go to open the lid when my phone blares to life next to me.

Bugs goes flying as my limbs flail in fright.

"Fuck!" I yelp, grabbing my phone and silencing the call.

It's Josh.

AGAIN.

The asshole has called eight times since last night. I haven't answered or read the seventeen messages I have from him. He probably thinks I'm still going to pound town with some random.

I reject the call, putting the phone on the duvet. My heart is hammering against my rib cage, and I mentally curse myself for being a wuss.

It's just a vibrator.

Slowly, I pick up Bugs again, and pull him out of the box. He feels light in my hands, the pink shade matching my cheeks. I press the on button, my eyes widening a little when it whirls to life. The shaft starts spinning, and I stare at the ears, watching them wiggle back and forth.

I test out a few different modes, before ditching my jeans and underwear. My fingers gracefully part my bits, the tips stroking myself how I normally would. I'm inexperienced, but I know straight away that Bugs isn't going inside of me unless I'm fully *prepared*.

My fingers dip inside my pussy, slowly, as my body hums. I feel a sense of pride as my fingers get coated with my wetness, and I bite my lip to hold back moans. I have no idea how soundproof the walls are, but I'm not particularly in the mood for anyone to hear me, especially my travel companions.

When I'm confident my body is ready, I lay back, my spine moulding against the soft mattress and pillow behind me. I give Bugs one last look before sending him down south, my heart racing in anticipation. I press the vibrator against my entrance, taking small shallow breaths before slowly pushing it inside.

My body tenses a bit at the sensation, my pussy clenching around the beaded shaft. It's tight and a little uncomfortable, but not painful.

The prongs touch my skin, wiggling around my clit and I swear I stop breathing. The feeling is... overwhelming.

Fuck. Why did I wait so long to buy a damn vibrator?

I do a few test strokes, focusing on my body as I try to relax. It feels intense, my body reacting as I feel the usual pleasure start building inside.

My fingers fumble as I try to find the button, changing the speed. My head flops back as Bugs moves faster, and I'm unable to control the quiet moans that spill from my mouth. Between the feeling of being full and the stroking of my clit, my body is fast climbing towards the sweet release I know is coming.

Confidence starts to fill me as I fuck myself a little faster, and my eyes close as I fall down the rabbit hole. Quite literally.

I no longer care that I'm moaning, or that the sounds are growing in volume. I've just made a new best friend, and my brain is melting with each second that passes.

Bugs works hard, swirling and convulsing in and around my body, and very quickly, I shatter. A cry escapes my lips, my back arching off the mattress as I come hard.

I lay panting and shaking, my legs twitching like I have just run a marathon. I'm too terrified to move, while also wondering if my soul has left my body.

With trembling fingers, I turn Bugs off, pulling him out. He buzzes in victory, and I give him a little thumbs up, before dropping him on the bed.

Even with my melted mind and incoherent thoughts, I'm aware that my fingers will never be enough from here on out.

I'm laying with a stupid grin on my face, enjoying the post-orgasmic high, when a knock on the door sends me into another panic.

I flail, falling off the bed as I quickly look at my pants-less situation.

"Fuck," I hiss quietly, ripping on my underwear and jeans. A second knock sounds as I fumble with my button. "Just a minute!" I yell, rushing towards the door in shock.

I can't focus, let alone function right now, so I'm stressing about human interaction and wondering if "I *just fucked myself*" is written all over my face.

I pat down my hair before pulling the door open. I blink at Nate in surprise, forcing myself to smile as innocently as possible.

"Hey," I greet, crossing my arms. "What's up?"

Nate smiles, looking down at me. "Brax and I just wanted to see what you were up to. Tyler has run off to meet up with a chick, and we were thinking of heading to the shops. Wanna come?"

"Uh, yeah sure. I was going that way, anyway. I just need to put some shoes on and grab my phone and purse."

I leave the door open, as I quickly grab my boots and step into them. I'm so flustered that I don't hear him follow me in.

"Audrey?"

I jump a little, looking behind at him. His eyes are glancing towards the bed, and like a bucket of cold water being poured onto me, I follow his line of vision in slow motion. I already know what I'm going to see, but I'm praying I'm not that stupid or unlucky.

Bugs is laying proudly on the duvet, the little ears sticking up in mock celebration.

"Oh my fucking God," I blurt out, dashing to the bed and shoving him and the box under the pillow.

I keep my back to Nate for a few seconds, trying to quickly think of a lie that will explain the rogue vibrator, or perhaps wait for the floor to open up and swallow me.

"Uh..." I start, refusing to look at him. "It's not what it looks like."

Nate chuckles, making me turn to look at him. "Right."

We stand in silence, looking at each other. I'm busted, and we both know it. But still, I cling to the idea that I can salvage what little dignity I have left.

"I brought it for a friend," I offer, awkwardly smiling.

Nate's eyes light up as he resists the urge to laugh. "And you were just doing some quality control testing?"

My mouth pops open before closing again. There is no getting out of this.

Nate holds up a hand. "Don't worry about it. No judgement here. It's normal."

"Is it?" I ask before I can stop myself. This is not the reaction I was expecting.

"Of course it is. Besides, I won't tell if you don't."

I nod appreciatively. "Thanks, Nate. Let's just forget about this awkward encounter and go see Salem."

"You're more quiet than usual," Brax points out as we stroll down the street.

"Am I?" I ask, pretending to look at something in the opposite direction to him so that my blushing cheeks are out of view.

Nate says nothing on the other side of Brax, and I'm thankful for it. He hasn't mentioned this morning at all, and we've had a nice day shopping. I briefly separated from them to get my witch costume, which is in a bag in my right hand. I'm excited about the hunt tomorrow, and nothing can dampen that.

Brax leads us towards a liquor shop. "Yeah. Is that asshole still bothering you?"

I shake my head, giving him a smile. "No. He's not bothering me."

*Just the fact that Nate knows I got off this morning.*

The two of them stop, leaving me to walk a few steps ahead. I pause, looking at them in question.

"What's the bet I can get us some beer without being carded?"

I raise my eyebrows in surprise. "You're not 21 yet."

"No," confirms Brax. "But everyone says I look 25, so it's worth a shot."

Nate nods in agreement as I hesitate. "You want to drink?" I ask, trying to clarify what the actual plan is here.

Brax grins. "Don't you?"

I shrug sheepishly. "I guess. But, that's illegal."

"Come on, Aud. Live a little," Brax winks, before heading inside the shop.

Nate and I hang around outside awkwardly, the silence between us growing as images appear in my head of Bugs.

I shove them aside, doing my best to 'play it cool', as I pretend I'm not a little bit turned on by the thoughts.

I can feel Nate watching me, as I look at surrounding shops. Halloween decorations are everywhere... it's like Halloween on steroids. But I fucking love it.

I wait for him to speak, but he doesn't. His gaze just continues to burn metaphorical holes in the side of my head. I can't help but wonder what he's thinking about, but it's easier to stay quiet and naïve.

Footsteps catch my attention, followed by the ding of the door sensor, and I turn to see Brax walking out with a box of beer. My mouth pops open in surprise, as he grins at us.

"Time to party."

# Chapter 4

I'm four beers deep, and it's night time, yet I'm more awake and alive than I've felt in weeks.

We're in the cemetery of all places, sitting between tombstones and graves, surrounded by empty bottles of beer. The guys are leaning back, legs spread, as they take in the quiet atmosphere and peace. Peace... a weird concept to associate with death, but I guess that's why they call it resting in peace.

I'm more at home with the dead. Their silence provides some comfort for me, and for the first time in what feels like ages, I'm able to focus on the emotion that threatens to consume me.

Anger... hurt... betrayal... pain.

Yet, sometimes, if I'm being honest, I want the pain. I want to feel something other than numbness. I want to be reminded that I'm alive, and that I survived the break-up. I know I did. *I broke up with him.* The alternative was staying with a cheater who doesn't respect me. Or worse, giving him something that can never be taken back.

I guess the truth is I don't care how or when I lose my virginity. As long as it's not to Josh.

I just want to feel the rush, the adrenaline... like what I feel when watching a scary movie. I want to live on the high, so that when I come down it motivates me to chase it again.

Right now, I'm stuck in limbo, plagued by his calls and text messages.

"Audrey... stop pacing. You're making me dizzy," Brax says huskily, stopping me. I stare at the two of them on the ground, watching me with both concern and amusement.

We're drunk.

I was drunk at two beers, but the feeling of euphoria pushed me to keep going. And right now... I don't regret a thing.

"Sorry," I respond, sitting down. "I'm so pumped up. It makes me want to run, or get Bugs."

"Bugs?" Brax asks confused, and I quickly cover my mouth with my hand. They both watch on with confusion before I see recognition in Nate's eyes. I give him a warning look, a silent plea. He stays quiet, but the shared look is enough for Brax to pick up on our little secret.

Brax waves his hand. "Nope. None of that... spill. What am I missing out on here?"

I curse myself. Out loud. Because I'm a drunk dumbass who blurts out everything when I've been drinking. It's a blessing and a curse. Many deep and meaningful conversations have taken place on drunken nights, which is great when you're with friends. But not your brother's best friends.

Nate shakes his head. "Not my story."

"I wonder if there's any ghosts here," I say in a desperate attempt to change the subject. They see right through me so well that I may as well be a ghost.

"Cut the crap. Tell me, Aud. This is a no secret zone, and if you're drinking with me, you gotta talk the talk."

I cover my face with my hands. "Bugs is my friend."

My fingers part, giving me a glimpse of Brax's still confused face.

"Okay?"

"He's the ... buzzing type of friend. You know, the one I got yesterday at that shop."

Brax's expression turns to surprise, and his mouth drops open as he lets out an "ooh".

Awkward silence swirls between us before Brax shrugs. "Nothing wrong with fiddling the flesh flute. Or ... buzzing, I guess in your case. Besides, that was the whole point of us going shopping."

I grab my beer and take a large drink. "I can't believe I just told you that."

"Don't sweat it. We don't care. We all do it, and I assumed you would... make friends with Bugs. I just didn't expect you to name it."

I sheepishly smile at Brax. "Yeah, but you're Tyler's best friends. I shouldn't say this shit to you."

"So?" says Brax. "We're just guys. Guys jerk off all the time. Hell, I did it this morning."

My internal movie projector kick starts again, and I quickly look away, scared that they will see my brain conjuring up images of Brax pleasuring himself.

"Maybe we should change the subject?" I offer.

Brax chuckles. "I don't mind. In fact, I like it. Come on, tell us your deepest, darkest fantasy. I bet you have some."

I shake my head. "I can't."

"Why?" asks Nate, sipping his beer.

I can't do it. I'm scared they will never look at me the same. And it's not just because I'm their best friend's little sister. It's because even though I've never done it, I *do* have fantasies. But mine don't involve roses or Egyptian cotton sheets. They definitely aren't sunshine and rainbows.

They are dark, twisted thoughts. Fucked up, even for a little, inexperienced virgin.

And it scares me that I'm not normal because of it.

They see the hesitation and worry on my face, passing me another beer. Nate's fingers brush against my hand as I take it from him. His touch leaves the feeling of static on my skin, my body buzzing from the alcohol. Or the thoughts consuming me.

This is a bad idea, but there's a part of me that wants to explore it.

"It's messed up," I finally say quietly. "I'm messed up."

Brax sits up straighter, staring at me intensely. "No, you're not. And unless it's fucking a corpse or a goat, then I'm certain it's not a bad thing."

I look down at the beer in my hand, and before I know it, I'm chugging back the whole thing in one go. Immediately, in my already too-far gone state, I'm losing a rational battle and feel the words forming before I can stop them.

"I want someone to take control. Fight me... scare me. I want it to hurt so that I feel everything. I want a little bit of pain and fear. I just want someone to fuck me like I'm not some young, broken-hearted girl. I want them to see me as their equal, *enough* to handle them. I want to be marked and tormented so that I know I'm theirs..."

The words fly out so quickly that I'm not even sure if this is reality anymore. Every depraved, dark thought I've kept locked up, is begging to come out.

Nate breaks the silence by letting out a long breath. "That's intense. But fucking hot."

"Yeah," Brax responds in agreement.

The cemetery is spinning now, almost as fast as my mind. "Well, fucking Joshua was never going to be it. There's probably a subconscious reason I never wanted to have sex with him. Maybe I knew all along what a slimy pathetic specimen he was."

They choke on their beers, giving me an amused look. I stare back at them wide-eyed. "What?"

Brax and Nate share a look before the latter speaks up. "Fuck him. You deserve better. Find someone who will treat you right, make you scream, and feel frustrated for the right reasons."

I snort, and before I can stop myself, I'm blurting out more words.

"What? Like you?"

I give a little laugh, slightly put-off by the fact they aren't laughing with me. Maybe I've gone too far.

My ass shuffles on the ground uncomfortably as I look around. "Sorry. Did you want to head back?"

Brax sighs, bringing my attention back to him.

"If we weren't drunk right now, I'd show you *exactly* what Nate means."

My heart misses a beat as I try to decipher if I heard him correctly.

"What do you mean?"

He shrugs. "I'd push you back against Steven McKing's tombstone there, rip off your pants, and make you scream so loud with my tongue that you wake the dead."

My eyes widen, and I hastily look at Nate for his reaction. To my surprise, he nods in agreement, his gaze off in the distance, as if we're just discussing the weather.

I have no idea what is happening right now. I shouldn't be sitting here drinking with them while Tyler is out on a date, and I definitely shouldn't be saying what comes out of my mouth next.

"I'd probably let you."

Two sets of eyes land on me, and I'd pay a pretty price to know what is going on in their heads right now. I've definitely gone too far, my legs moving as I ready myself to stand. It's time to call it a night, even though my mind is suddenly crystal clear. I no longer feel the effects of the alcohol, my sobriety returning quickly as realization settles in.

Before I can stand though, a hand falls onto my leg halting me. My eyes follow the arm, travelling up until I've found Brax's face. His green eyes are watching me carefully, assessing my reaction. I'm like a deer in headlights, frozen in place.

"You would let us?" he asks slowly. "You would let me fuck you with my mouth, erasing all memories of that asshole, until all you can think of is how hard you've come for me?"

Our eyes are locked, and I'm still so intensely aware of his hand on my leg. His fingers dig in a little, pressing down onto my thigh through my jeans.

I nod slowly, swallowing hard. "Yes."

I watch with bated breath as Brax leans forward, his lips grazing the side of my neck. My eyes flutter closed as my body trembles, and a rush of heat races to my stomach. His hand slides up my leg, finding my waist, as his other hand threads through my hair. I gasp as he suddenly grabs a handful of my hair, pulling my head sideways harshly. My eyes shoot open, locking with Nate's, who is watching on with heated interest.

Brax's lips reach my ear, his breath making me shiver as he gently kisses my earlobe.

"I respect you too much to take advantage of you right now. But mark my words. If we cross paths again in the dark, you better run. Because we will catch you, and when we're finished with you, we're going to ruin you in the best way possible."

# Chapter 5

Halloween.

It's finally here.

I should be excited, and in theory, I am. But I'm also caught up in the whirlwind of fuckery that was last night.

After stumbling home like a penguin off it's face, I woke this morning replaying conversations from the cemetery last night. My brain indicates that Brax and Nate nearly devoured me against a tombstone, but the hangover suggests that maybe I was imagining things. Or perhaps I took it out of context.

Either way, I'm hiding out in my room today until the Witch Hunt starts tonight.

As far as I'm aware, the three guys have plans elsewhere all day, so I'll be safe. The only thing I'll need to watch out for is demons and hunters trying to catch me tonight.

My phone buzzes on the bed next to me, and I resist stabbing myself in the eye at the sight of Josh's name. I'm well and truly over this shit. I can feel the momentum growing in me, threatening to snap what little patience I have left. My hand grabs the phone, swiping the accept button.

"What?!" I yell down the phone, much to the surprise of the recipient.

"Jesus, Audrey! What the fuck?"

I sigh aggressively, my fingers clenching the cool metal firmly. "What the fuck do you want, Joshua? Stop goddamn calling me."

"Babe, firstly... what the fuck is your problem? Secondly, if you had picked up the phone the first hundred times I called, it wouldn't be an issue."

Is this fuckhead for real?

"Josh, my problem is you. Or, it was. Now, you're nothing to me. So fuck off, and go back to banging Carly on your mom's porcelain set."

I hear him gasp, and a sense of pride fills me. He splutters for a moment before regaining himself.

"You're one to talk! Out fucking randoms. I obviously meant nothing to you. Maybe you weren't even a virgin."

I can just imagine his smug face, thinking his insult has hit me where it hurts. Maybe he wants me to cry, or beg for him back. But that won't happen. Not now, not ever.

"Sorry you feel that way, Joshua. Take your four inches and fuck off elsewhere. Bye now."

His yelling is cut off by the end call button. I quickly switch my phone off, laying back with a deep sigh. I'll never let someone treat me like that again. At the end of the day, I know my worth, and my beliefs. I don't need a boyfriend for the sake of it, and if I end up being the only virgin at college next Fall, then so be it.

Though, if my hormones have anything to say about it... I don't think that will happen. Bugs was one thing, but Brax teasing me last night... I'm in trouble. It just makes me want to explore my kinks more. However, I'm now under the impression that my drunken mind imagined a lot of last night. There's no way they want to ravish me.

But that doesn't mean a girl can't dream.

Salem is buzzing tonight. Everywhere I look, people are dressed up in costumes. Some are trick or treating, others are just walking around exploring.

I end up following a group that's heading towards the city's edge, to the makeshift maze that's been created.

The Witch Hunt kicks off at 6:30pm, just after the city gets covered in darkness. Little bits of light are still creeping around, but slowly, the shadows are taking over.

The maze is huge, weaving in and out of trees, guarded by large blocks. The blocks are a various mixture of wood, stone, brick, and cement. Some are covered in fake blood and spray paint, giving the illusion of danger. I suppose in a way, it is dangerous. Those of us who have opted to be witches are going to be hunted and chased. There's lots of places to hide in the woods and behind structures, but there's also a lot of open space.

As I approach the sign-in tent, my heart starts racing with excitement. It's like a real horror movie coming to life. Predators are waiting together on one side, and it's a sight to be seen. Devils, Freddy Kruegers, Michael Myers, and Chucky Dolls are packed together. Some have weapons... fake knives and chainsaws, and they tauntingly sneer at witches as they pass. I can hear the pretend threats and promises from the hunters, and a few witches hesitate, questioning whether they want to participate after all.

I'm ready.

They can hunt me all they like.

I head up to the sign-in table, giving the person on the other side a smile. The guy in his 20s is dressed like Lucifer Morningstar, except half of his face is in devil form. He grins at me in return, pushing a piece of paper towards me.

"Hiya, babe. Please read and sign this liability waiver. If you're not familiar with the rules, there's a board over to your right. But in a nutshell, you guys will get a five minute head start. The hunt will last two hours, but you can leave at any time. If you're captured and dragged back to the stakes, it's game over. No violence or over the top physical touch allowed from participants, and you must stay in the designated maze at all times."

Nodding, I scribble my name on the paper before handing it back. In return, he gives me a wrist band that glows in the dark. He helps tie it onto my wrist before crossing my name off a list.

"Best of luck to you, babe."

"Thanks," I laugh, moving away from the table to wait with the other witches.

As I stand in the pack, my gaze can't help wandering over the hunters. There's more of us than them so that's helpful, but it doesn't mean it's going to be easy. Two hours is a long time, and the hunters don't have a limit on how many witches they can capture to 'burn'.

Someone yells out that there's five minutes until the start, earning jeers from the hunters and a few screams from the witches. I can't help but grin stupidly in excitement.

A gap parts on the hunters side, and my eyes are drawn to a man standing in the middle of the pack. He's shirtless, his exposed muscles rippling above low hanging jeans. He's wearing a blue neon skull mask, the lights flashing but that's not just what has my attention. His torso and arms are dripping in fake blood. Even though I can't see his eyes, I get the eerie feeling he's watching me. Slowly, he turns to someone next to him and I spot another guy. The second man is wearing an orange neon mask, dressed the same in just jeans and fake blood.

It's a huge contrast to my own costume. I'm in a black, fitted summer playsuit, with a sewed on lacy cape. I've done my makeup a dark, smoky-eye style with dark red lips and worn all-black Converse shoes for comfort... and running purposes. My hair is Dutch braided, the red sticking out against the black outfit. I tried my best to dress for flexibility, unlike some of the others here, who are in long black dresses with traditional pointy hats.

There's no doubt in my mind now that the two of them are watching me. It's pretty obvious, because the one in blue lifts his bloodied hand, and makes a slashing motion across his neck my way. My heart stops and my mouth feels dry, and I suddenly feel like there's a target on my back. I can't see who they are, but it's clear they are coming for me.

Before I can even ponder that thought, a loud voice erupts over a speakerphone.

"Witches! Make your way to the start line. It's time."

# Chapter 6

My feet shuffle backwards as I start to move with the crowd around me, but my eyes are still locked on the two men. My excitement has temporarily evaporated. All I feel now is fear, my heart pounding, as I prepare myself to run into the dark maze ahead.

Finally, I break eye contact, pushing past other participants to stand near the start. I'm hoping to get as far into the maze as I can before the five minute head start is up.

Suddenly, a row of posts on either side of the start line ignite in flames, the torches illuminating our faces and the bodies of the officials as they watch us. Off to the side, there's makeshift stakes set up, and I'm even more determined not to end up there.

The voice comes over the speaker again, drowning out the chatter around me.

"Good luck, witches. Run fast."

A siren rings out, reminding me of The Purge. Immediately, my body takes off into a sprint. Screams sound out around me as other people head into the maze. About 300 feet into the maze, it breaks off into multiple directions. There's no indication of what might lie ahead, so I just choose a random entry point. People around me scatter, everyone going in different directions, as we hurriedly attempt to put distance between us and the hunters.

My path changes constantly as I'm met with multiple blocks, obstacles and turns. I try to pick random pathways, throwing myself in deeper. The further I go, the darker it gets. There's a few torches and flames lighting up the maze, but for the most part, we're in darkness. My eyes struggle to adjust at first, but I stay determined. I start looking around at objects, assessing the area for hiding places. I know logically there's no way I'm going to be able to run non-stop for two hours, so my best plan is to run, then hide, then keep going.

In the distance, I hear a second siren, signalling the hunters entering the maze. Their faint shouts and cheers make my stomach feel hollow, and I know it's only a matter of time before the faster ones reach this section.

I notice some hollow, plastic road barricades and run over. I inspect the top, and smile triumphantly when I see it unclips. I make quick work of opening the top, climbing inside, and pulling the lid shut as I squeeze my body in the small space.

It's a risky move because when I choose to go to another spot, it's going to be difficult to get out inconspicuously. There's a tiny hole in the side and I inch closer, peeking out. It's a narrow view, but I can just see enough to use it as a way to check if the coast is clear.

Screams are breaking out left, right and center as people are caught. It's terrifying because slowly, but surely, the sounds get louder as the hunters get deeper into the maze.

Footsteps run past the barricade, making my heartrate speed up. People are panicking, trying to hide or outrun the hunters.

I peek through the hole, covering my mouth to hide any sounds, as I spot the first lot of hunters step into my section. A group of guys dressed in Scream masks survey the area, one of them holding a fake chainsaw. At least, I hope it's fake. Props to companies for making Halloween shit look so realistic.

A whimper breaks out in the shrubs behind my hiding spot. The guys simultaneously turn towards it, before two of them rush forward. There's the sound of commotion before a scream is let loose. My eyes widen and I crouch lower, willing myself to take small, silent breaths.

I move away from the hole, but I can still see a small preview. Bodies walk past, dragging someone between them. The witch is fighting back, but it's no use. She's been captured.

The small group cheer amongst themselves, and the sound of their footsteps leaving the section bring me a wave of relief.

It goes silent again but not for long, as more hunters pass the area every few minutes.

I decide it's time to get ready to move, and shuffle closer to the hole to check. It sounds quiet, so I'm fairly confident no one is around. I peer out, and let out a silent gasp when I find the guys in neon masks standing in the pathway looking around. There's no words being exchanged between them but they're communicating silently.

I quickly move away from the hole, careful not to make any noise as I listen. I can't even tell if they are moving. They are so quiet and precise in their footsteps... like real predators.

Against my better judgement, I look again, finding the section empty. I have no idea where they have gone, and I could stay and wait, but each minute that passes, I'm more and more at risk of being found.

Carefully, I lift the barricade lid, popping my head out. There's no one around, and I breathe a sigh of relief. I climb out, making sure I don't make any sounds.

Putting the lid back, I look around. There's two pathways further into the maze. The likelihood of hunters being down both is high, but I go with my gut, and take the left one.

It's dark, and I'm thankful for the ground being soft. It's helping mask my footsteps.

As I reach another section of crossroads, I swing a right this time, taking me along the outskirts of the maze. It's so eerily quiet that it's unsettling. I can still hear people being found further away, but it seems almost too lucky to be this deserted.

I quickly take a look at my phone, noting I've been in the maze for 30 minutes. It's only been a quarter of the time, but it feels longer.

The path continues, and I duck behind a shrub when I hear footsteps start heading towards me. I peer through the gap, finding a sole hunter dressed as Freddy Krueger checking the area. He can't see me thankfully, and takes off to another section.

There's not many places to hide in this part, so I go to the opposite option, and head away from Freddy.

A few minutes pass, and I find myself at a clearing. The section is on the edge of the maze, signs indicating that the other side of the wall is out of bounds. In the corners there's some boulders, and what appears to be nooses hanging from trees. It's much darker in this section, so I squint my eyes while looking around to see through the shadows.

A rustling noise in the corner behind me catches my attention, and I quickly turn around. I can't see anything, but I can feel it. I'm being watched. All I can do is hope and pray that it's a witch in hiding. That would make sense, right? Because a hunter would charge forward to try to grab me.

I stare at the black corner for a few more seconds, but there are no more noises. I try to convince myself that I'm just hearing things, despite the fact I can still feel eyes on me.

Turning away from the corner, I go back to looking at the options to leave this section. As I take a step towards the one closest to me, a branch snapping behind me stops me in my tracks. I twist my head slowly, staring at the dark corner again.

Without a shadow of a doubt, I'm not alone. But the question is... friend or foe?

My feet inch towards the exit of the section, as my eyes stay focused on the unknown. Suddenly, the silence is broken by a click, and I watch in horror as I find myself staring at the now-lit neon blue skull mask.

Another click sounds behind me from the adjacent corner, and I swing around to find the orange skull mask illuminating in the darkness.

I'm standing between them, frozen as I try to figure out my next move. A dark whispered chuckle breaks the silence, and immediately, I spring into action, rushing forward towards the exit. The sound of their footsteps ring out behind me as they give chase, and I push myself to run as fast as possible.

Panic fills me as I weave in and out of the maze, no longer able to keep track of where I'm going. Their sinister laughter behind me gets closer, and I desperately try to find salvation.

I pass other hunters and witches, but no one bothers to try to catch me. Why would they bother when I'm being stalked by two men covered in blood?

As I reach the other side of the maze, I gasp as I find myself at a dead end. I quickly stumble back, ready to turn and run, but a body collides with me, knocking us both to the ground. A groan escapes through my lips and I flip onto my back. Strong hands pin my arms by my head, and I'm frozen in fear as I stare up at blue-face.

I fight against his grip, my much smaller body no match for his strength. From behind, I spot his friend approaching slowly, like a lion stalking it's wounded prey.

The neon lights get closer as my capturer leans down. His bare chest rubs against mine, the blood coating my own skin and clothes, and making him slide against me easily.

I gasp again as the other guy drags a plastic barricade over the entrance to our little dead end, followed by another on top, creating a block.

"What are you doing?" I ask in a panic, struggling against the arms pinning me down.

They don't respond, and this time my fear is real. I'm trapped. And there's nothing I can do.

An orange glow is cast over my face, and I stare up at the two of them now leaning over me. Orange-face reaches into his pants pocket, extracting something. I look at it, trying to figure out what I'm staring at, before recognition hits me.

It's duct tape and red rope.

# Chapter 7

I stop struggling and look at them in disbelief.

"Brax? Nate?" I ask with a shaky voice.

"Trick or treat, Red..." comes the familiar voice of Brax from behind the blue mask.

Nate hands over the duct tape to Brax, who rips a strip away from the roll. He lifts his mask temporarily, using his teeth to rip the tape off.

"Any time you want to stop, all you have to do is tap your hand or foot three times," Brax murmurs huskily.

Before I can respond, he shoves the piece of tape over my mouth. I stare at him with wide eyes but make no move to tap out, my arms still by my head even though they aren't being held down anymore.

Brax lowers his mask back down as he continues straddling my waist. Nate moves forward, coming to stand behind my head. He grabs my wrists, binding them together with the red rope that I recognize from the adult shop.

I try to talk to ask them what's going on, but it's muffled by the tape. Nate shushes me gently, his hand sliding down my tied arms to rest on my neck.

"You can stop us at any time," he reminds me. "But, we did promise you that you would be ours if we caught you. And we fully plan on keeping that promise."

Brax reaches into his pocket and pulls out a switch-blade. "Do you trust us, babe?"

My eyes flicker between him and the knife. Is he seriously asking if I trust them while I am tied up and helpless with a knife pointing at me?

Surprisingly, the answer comes easy.

I nod, watching him carefully. My nodding is halted as Nate presses down on my throat, his hand pushing into the delicate flesh and cutting off my air supply. I let out a silent gasp, any sounds captured by the tape and the pressure around my throat. The action sends shivers coursing through my body. My legs press together as I feel my body responding to their touch.

"I can't wait to taste you. It's been on my mind since the cemetery last night," Brax murmurs, flicking open the switchblade. With his free hand, he runs it over my body, stopping to squeeze my breasts through my playsuit. I arch up into his touch, meeting resistance as Nate puts more pressure against my throat. I can barely breathe and it should scare me, yet all I can think about is how much I want it.

Brax reaches the apex of my thighs, his hand rubbing my sex through the thin material that separates us. I moan, the tiny sound vibrating against Nate's hand.

"I bet she's getting so wet for us," remarks Nate, watch-ing Brax's movements. The latter hums in agreement, pulling the material across to expose my pussy. His index finger glides gently along my slit, dipping ever so slightly inside.

"She's dripping already," he says, swirling around my arousal. "Our good little slut."

My pride flies out the window at his comment, my inner demons fighting to come out. I suddenly have the urge to want to please them, to hear all their praises.

Brax's finger pushes deeper, finding its way into my eager body. It's a foreign feeling but not uncomfortable.

"Jesus, she's fucking clenching me so tight," Brax says, adding a second finger.

I whimper against the tape as he starts moving his fingers in and out of my body. My hips work up a rhythm, pushing greedily against his hand. I let out a muffled cry as he suddenly removes his hand, leaving me feeling empty and begging for more.

He tips his mask up, locking eyes with me, as he slips his fingers into his mouth.

"So sweet. The perfect Halloween treat."

Brax moves further down, forcefully spreading my legs apart. He trails the knife up my thigh, the tip promising pain as it glides over my skin. As he reaches my playsuit, he pulls it away from my body, slashing the material with the knife. I feel the playsuit and my underwear rip, exposing me to him completely.

My legs are thrown over his shoulders as he leans down, his nose brushing against my inner thighs. "Ours," he whispers, before shoving his tongue between my folds. My body jolts like it's been zapped by electricity, making Nate squeeze down on my throat harder. Nate leans down, kissing the duct tape over my mouth. I try to kiss him back, whimpering when I can't.

Brax's hands spread my folds, holding me open as his tongue attacks my clit. Little balls of light are appearing in my vision, and I'm not sure if it's from the lack of oxygen, or the pleasure ripping through my body.

In the distance, I can hear screams and footsteps, as people pass by our little closed off section. My heart stammers as I wonder if we'll be caught. But then I realize, I don't fucking care. Let them all see.

Fingers gently find their way into my eager body, but his tongue never stops. I clench my legs around his head, holding him greedily as he fucks me with his mouth.

I can feel my body tensing up, the promise of release coming. Brax's fingers move faster, and I barely notice Nate remove his hand from my throat. Instead, he pins down my arms above my head, holding me still as I wiggle helplessly. I'm chasing the high and as I feel the familiar sensation of my orgasm approaching, Brax suddenly releases me.

I protest through the tape, watching him pull back with a smirk on his face.

"Easy, babe. You'll come when I say you come."

My eyes widen in disappointment and disbelief, my body screaming in pain, as my pussy throbs desperately for relief. Brax holds the knife up, little specks of light reflecting off the silver blade. He trails the sharp tip up my thighs, and I gasp when he suddenly digs a little deeper. My skin stings from the cut, making my sex ache more.

He repeats the motion on my other thigh, drawing blood which drips slowly down my thighs. I look down, mesmerized as it mixes with the fake blood already on my skin.

Nate releases my arms, holding his hand out to Brax. In a silent exchange, Brax hands over the knife, moving out of the way so Nate can take his place.

As Nate settles between my thighs, his face looks over Brax's handiwork, a smirk pulling at his lips.

"You bleed so well for us. I bet you come even better."

I watch in confusion and fascination as he turns the knife around, the blade resting in his palm. I suck in a breath as he runs the hard handle up and down my slit, teasing me.

Nate gives me a taunting grin, lifting his mask. His eyes dance like flames as he slowly pushes the handle inside of me. My body tenses up, and Brax runs his hands down my arms, continuing to trail them down the side of my body. I instantly relax into his touch before feeling the handle move further inside of me. Nate pulls it back slightly, repeating the motion as he fucks me with the knife.

"That's a good girl. I want you to come on our knife," he whispers, his thumb drawing circles around my clit.

I'm already on the edge from being teased by Brax, that my orgasm starts building quickly again. Nate fucks me faster, his thumb pressing down on my sensitive clit.

The world around me is falling into pieces. Brax leans forward, ripping the duct tape off my mouth quickly. My skin tingles from the pain, and mixed with the feeling of being filled, my climax rips through me. Brax covers my mouth, capturing my cries as he kisses me.

As I come down from the high, the knife handle is pulled out of my body.

"Fucking hell. You're perfect, Audrey," Nate murmurs, stroking my folds. "I can't wait to feel you around my cock."

I take a breath as Brax pulls back from kissing me. "Do it," I beg, my voice shaking.

The two of them share a look before Nate's hands grab my hips. He flips me onto my stomach, putting my head in Brax's lap. My tied hands rest on his chest, and I bury my head into his pants. I can see his cock straining through the fabric, showing me just how much they want me.

It's a powerful feeling, knowing that I'm making them feel exactly what they are doing to me.

Nate's fingers dig into my hips, pulling me back roughly so my ass is in the air.

"I can't wait to ruin you."

I can feel him undoing his pants behind me, his cock breaking free to rest on my bare skin. He grips his length, running the head up and down my slit.

Brax strokes my cheek gently before grabbing a fistful of my hair and ripping my head back to look at him. The mask is still tilted up and we lock eyes.

"Keep your eyes on me. I want to see your face as Nate takes your innocence."

Nate's hand gently strokes my ass and I gasp as I feel the head of his cock pushing up against my entrance. It's finally happening and my fear has suddenly returned. It's clearly written on my face because Brax cups my cheeks.

"Deep breaths. You've got this," he says, giving me an encouraging smile.

He nods at Nate behind me, and I feel his cock slowly pushing inside. I bite my lip as I stretch around him. There's no pain, only the sensation of foreign discomfort as I adjust to his invasion.

"Good girl," Brax whispers, holding my gaze. "Fuck, look at how well you're taking him. Just like we knew you would."

Nate pauses when he's fully inside me, giving me a moment to get used to the new feeling. He squeezes my ass. "You feel amazing, Audrey. It's taking all my willpower not to fuck you senseless."

I move my hips curiously, my hands curling into fists against Brax's chest. "More," I plead.

He pulls back slightly before sheathing himself fully in me again. We both groan in unison, and he continues, repeating the movement. Nate starts moving, going a little faster and deeper with each thrust.

My eyes close on their own accord and I feel my hair being gripped and ripped back again.

"Eyes on me, Aud," Brax commands. "Or I'll have to punish you."

"How?" I ask with a whisper, fighting the urge to bury my head in his lap.

Brax's lips tilt up into a smirk. "I'll have to fuck your mouth."

My pussy clenches around Nate, making him groan. "Do it," he says to Brax, thrusting a little harder. "She can take it."

Brax looks at me for confirmation, and I hesitate for a second before giving a small nod.

"Jesus, you'll be the fucking death of me," he says, reaching down to unbutton his pants. I watch as he frees his cock, his hand sliding over the tip as he starts stroking himself. It's so close to my face, so near that I can see the perfect bead of pre-cum sitting on the tip, begging to be licked.

Brax grips the back of my head while holding his length in the other. "Do you want my cock?"

I nod eagerly, and he responds by pushing the head against my lips, prompting me to open. Nate slows down, allowing me the chance to taste Brax at my own speed.

Experimentally, I take my time moving around his cock, moaning against his shaft as I work him into my mouth. It's new to me but his groans encourage me, as his hand gently pushes me lower to take more.

I get into a bit of a rhythm and almost forget Nate is still inside of me, waiting for his turn. His hand comes down on my ass cheek, slapping me.

"I hope you're ready. Because now, we're going to have some real fun."

# Chapter 8

I start to pull away from Brax but Nate suddenly edges back, before thrusting in deep. I let out a gasp, my nails digging into Brax's chest as I force myself to stay focused. They are both in me and I tilt my head up to look at Brax. My eyes ask the question, but I only receive a smug smile in reply.

Nate starts fucking me hard and I cry out, the sound muffled by Brax's cock in my mouth. The hand on my head steadies me, as he works his cock in and out of my mouth.

"That's it, baby. Take us both," Brax says, his eyes on my face.

My nails dig into his chest again, this time hard enough to draw blood. He hisses, but makes no move to remove them, instead leaning into my touch more.

I'm not even sure where I start and they end, the three of us joined, as the two of them fuck my bound body.

Nate's arm wraps around my hip, his fingers reaching around to find my clit. My body trembles as he rubs his fingers over it.

"Come for me, Aud," he commands, stroking me faster.

To my surprise, my body obeys, a shattering orgasm ripping through me out of nowhere. He continues pounding me through it, dragging out the pleasure as I shake and struggle to hold myself upright.

Suddenly, I feel Nate pull out of me. Brax follows suit and I barely have time to look at him questioningly before I'm rolled onto my back.

Nate straddles my body, moving up so his wet cock is above my face.

"Open your mouth," he demands, stroking his length aggressively.

I immediately comply, and he leans forward, putting the tip in between my lips. He keeps stroking, placing one hand next to my head to steady himself.

I feel something hit the back of my throat, and I watch in fascination as he groans, his eyes shutting. His release pools in my mouth and I wait as he finishes.

Nate shuffles back slightly, leaning down to grab my chin. He pushes my mouth closed, kissing it.

"Swallow me."

There's a brief hesitation, but I quickly swallow so I can kiss him back. I want more of him, of them both.

Nate swings his leg over, moving off me as he does his pants up. He picks me up, straddling me over Brax's lap, who is stroking his length while watching me.

"Put your arms around my head," Brax says and I do, the end of the rope dangling down his bare back.

Nate's hands grip the outer sides of my thighs, forcing me to spread open.

"Sit down on his cock."

I lower myself down, my mouth popping open as he enters me at my own pace. Nate grabs my hips, lifting me up and down Brax's cock. "Like that, Aud. Ride him."

Brax leans forward, our lips smashing together. I do as they say, moving my hips as Nate helps hold my weight. Brax leans back on his hands, pushing his hips up into me. I moan as he goes deeper, hitting the sweet spot inside me.

Nate lets go of my hips, grabbing my arms to remove them from Brax's neck. He lifts them above my head, pulling them back so they are against his own chest. Nate pins my arms against him, and leans down to pick up the knife next to us.

He drags it along my chest, the pointy tip leaving little red marks on my flustered skin. When it reaches the center of my breasts, he pushes the tip into my skin harder while dragging the blade down. Small droplets of blood follow, dripping down my chest and falling onto my stomach. It's not a huge cut, maybe only an inch, but it feels like my soul is leaving my body through the wound.

I'm going straight to Hell with a first class ticket.

Nate throws the knife aside, his finger collecting the droplets of blood as he smears it back up my body. His finger trails over the cut gently, a bloody path following as he grabs my throat.

He tilts my head back, forcing me to look up at him from behind.

"You look so beautiful when in ruins."

Nate leans over, kissing me, as Brax thrusts harder, upwards into my body. I feel fingers graze my clit, pinching and stroking it as my moans are swallowed by Nate.

My body freezes as another orgasm surprises me. I hear one of them whisper "good girl", but I'm too lost to figure out who it is.

I can't see anything, my vision shades of white and grey from my release.

Arms lift me off Brax, and my knees hit the soft ground. I'm dizzy, like I've been underwater and am now taking my first breaths of sweet air.

A hand holds my throat, steadying me.

"Open up," Nate whispers, his other hand flat against my décolletage.

Slowly, things come back to life, the white vanishing and Brax appearing in its place. He's standing in front of me, waiting.

My mouth opens as our eyes meet and he steps forward, pushing his cock inside. I moan on his length. I can taste myself on him, the mixture of our bodies sending me into a frenzy.

There's no gentle control this time. Instead, Brax grabs the top of my head, fisting a handful of hair. He fucks my mouth at his desired pace, forcing me to adjust to his length and speed.

Nate's still holding my throat, keeping me still, and I'm at their mercy as they take control.

I taste Brax's release, his hands moving to grip the sides of my face as he holds me still while he pours himself into my mouth. I choke a little, willing myself to be calm and swallow. After I do, he pulls out slowly, his cock falling from my lips.

My breathing is ragged, and I feel my knees give out. I fall back onto my calves as gentle hands stroke my hair.

Someone sits down behind me, pulling me slowly into their lap. I let out a small breath as the pressure is taken off my legs. Quick hands make work of the rope, freeing my wrists.

"Are you okay?" Nate says, his arms wrapping around my body.

I nod, unable to speak yet. Brax does his pants up, kneeling down in front of me. His green eyes check my face for any signs of concern or discomfort, but there's none. Just a level of exhaustion I didn't know existed.

In the distance, a siren rings out, alerting us to the end of the witch hunt.

"We better head out before they come looking," Brax says, sneaking a glance at the plastic barricades blocking the entrance.

"Can you walk?" Nate asks.

I wiggle my legs, straightening them out. "I think so," I answer quietly, moving to stand.

Brax stands up, reaching to grab my hands. He helps pull me to my feet, holding them as I take a second to ground myself.

My hands flatten down my playsuit, which has now turned into a dress. When they are confident I'm not going to fall over, they let me go, pulling their masks back down. They work together to move the barricades, pocketing the duct tape and rope.

As we step out of our little dead end, we pass a few people making their way back towards the maze entrance. It's mostly hunters, but a few witches appear, grins on their faces at having survived.

When we reach the entrance, there's a small group of people chatting. I notice a bunch of witches standing by the stakes. They were caught, and are now waiting for their time to 'burn'.

The three of us huddle together in silence, waiting as the last of the people in the maze emerge.

Lucifer Morningstar stands up on a barricade with a speakerphone in his hand.

"Ladies and Gentlemen, your hard work has paid off. These witches have been caught, and will now pay for their sins."

I glance at the stakes, noticing fake LED lights surrounding each of them. The witches stand at the stakes, loosely tied up as people approach. Simultaneously, the LED lights are switched on, giving the illusion of fire surrounding their feet.

The hunters in the crowd cheer, while the witches laugh enjoying the attention.

I guess I can relate. It definitely wasn't bad being caught at all.

# Chapter 9

---

I let out a hiss as the hot water hits my skin. The pain quickly vanishes, my body sagging under the water as I lean against the wall.

The walk back from the hunt had been quiet. The three of us were silent, but it didn't feel awkward. At least, not entirely.

As I come down from my high, I'm left with feelings of confusion. I don't really expect anything from Nate and Brax, but we're now in a grey zone.

What are we? Friends? Lovers?

Or will they just be the tale of how I lost my virginity? The girl who slept with her brother's best friends during the vacation...

I climb out of the shower, wrapping myself in the fluffy white towel. I'm careful to make sure no blood, fake or real, gets on it.

My phone dings from the bed, but I ignore it. It's probably Joshua, having his usual complaint. And right now, he doesn't get to ruin this feeling. I just lost my virginity in the most delish way, on my favorite day of the year. He doesn't exist in my world, and I'll be damned if I let him take this from me.

I stop in front of the mirror in my room looking at myself. I don't look any different, except for the marks and cuts that Nate and Brax inflicted on me. My finger traces the cut on my chest, a small smile appearing on my face as I remember the thrill of being chased, then the pleasure that followed.

I'm so exhausted that I can't even be bothered getting dressed. Instead, I drop the towel, pulling back the duvet to climb in naked. The sheets feel like heaven against my skin, and I can't fight sleep even if I wanted to. It consumes me immediately, and I fall into a world of dreams containing neon masks and red rope.

"Audrey! Open up. Check-out is in half an hour and I don't want to be late!"

I sit up in a fright, the sheet falling from my body as I look around wildly. A fist pounds on the door, and I rub my eyes, the light blinding me.

"Just a minute!" I yell, and hear Tyler groan in frustration.

"Seriously?!" he shouts back. "Honestly, if you're not ready by 10am, I'm leaving without you."

I hear his footsteps walk away, and I fall back onto the bed with a groan.

Is it still murder if I have a reasonable excuse?

I shift uncomfortably, dragging myself from the bed. My whole body aches, including between my legs, but the feeling is incredible. The only downside is having to spend four hours in the car with my brother and the two guys who now have my V card.

The possibility of taking a train home stops me for a second, but I decide against it. Running away like a scared little girl won't change the fact I got banged last night. Besides, that will only lead to questions from Tyler, Brax, Nate, and our parents.

I pack my stuff, shoving it back into my suitcase, get dressed and make it downstairs by 9:55am. Tyler is standing in the foyer, pacing. He stops when he catches sight of me.

"Finally. You never sleep in this late. Are you trying to stress me out?"

"Doesn't sound like something I would do," I mumble sarcastically, handing over my room key to Alex.

Tyler rolls his eyes. "Sure, it doesn't. What are baby sisters for, if not to annoy?"

*They are there to fuck your best friends.*

Brax and Nate are nowhere to be seen, and I ignore the feeling of disappointment. Tyler helps me with my stuff, leading us outside.

"I'm going to miss this place," he says, looking around.

I raise an eyebrow at him. "Really? You didn't do anything the whole time we were here."

"Didn't I?" he laughs, and I look at him suspiciously.

"Date went well, I take it?"

Tyler grins stupidly while fishing out his car keys from his back pocket. "Sure did. Francine might even come visit me at Thanksgiving."

I snort, and he glares at me.

"What?" he demands.

"Nothing," I offer, throwing a hand up. "Nothing at all."

We approach Tyler's car, and my heart skips a beat as I spot Brax and Nate waiting by the rear. They look at me and I quickly turn away, reaching for my belongings from Tyler.

"I've got it," says Tyler, pulling my suitcase away from me. "Just get in the car."

I pause for a moment, before nodding. I walk to the back passenger door, opening it and slipping inside. The others load the bags into the back, and I quickly set up my phone and AirPods, turning on music. Brax climbs into the seat next to me, staring at me quietly as I do my best to avoid looking at either of them.

Nate sits in the front passenger seat, sharing a quick look with Brax as I stare out the window. No one says anything thankfully, and Tyler climbs in with a sigh.

"Alright. Back to reality."

I fell asleep somewhere about half way home, my head perched against the window. The car stops with a jolt and I grab the seat in front of me.

"What the heck?" I mumble, half asleep.

"Uh, you have a visitor," Tyler says dryly.

I look around, noticing Brax staring at something outside the car. I follow his line of vision, finding Josh at the front of our house. His eyes zone in on the car, arms crossed as he waits for me.

"Fucking great," I murmur, unclipping my seatbelt.

"Maybe he wants to give you a second chance," Tyler chuckles. He's so full of himself that he misses the glare Nate and Brax send his way.

I lean forward and hit the back of Tyler's seat. "Not that it's any of your business, but I dumped him. For cheating on me."

"What?!" Tyler spins around in his seat, looking at me. The amusement has left his eyes, anger in its place. It doesn't matter how much we fight, I'm always going to be his baby sister. And despite his attitude towards me, he still gets protective.

"Yeah. So, now you know. Stay here, don't do anything stupid for once."

I open the car door, climbing out. Josh steps towards the car, watching me carefully. He probably assumes I'll try to run and hide, and ordinarily he'd be right. But something has shifted in me now. There was something about last night that changed and solidified things for me.

I walk up to Josh, my eyes glaring daggers at him. "What are you doing here?"

"You wouldn't return any of my calls or messages. We need to talk."

He runs his hand through his shaved black hair. He's nervous, but it's not for the reasons he would lead me to believe. He's just mad because he can't have his cake and eat it too. And because we had him believing someone else wanted me, he suddenly wants to give chase again. Boys always want what they can't have.

"Josh, we're done. Just let it go," I say, crossing my arms.

"Babe, I love you. I told you, it was an accident. I had a moment of weakness, but I'm here now, trying to make it right."

The sound of car doors closing behind me make me turn and look. Tyler is stalking up the pathway towards us, as Nate and Brax trail not far behind.

"Asshole, she said she doesn't want you here. Fuck off," Tyler says, coming to a stop next to me.

He's a good five inches taller than Josh, and intimidating as hell when he wants to be. Josh swallows before his ego takes a turn in the driver's seat.

"This doesn't concern you. It's between me and my girlfriend."

Tyler isn't fazed by his words, instead breaking out in a sarcastic laugh.

"Oh, really? Because it seems to me like she dumped your ass!"

I snort, covering my mouth, because up until five minutes ago, Tyler had no idea what the hell had even happened. Josh looks at me, his brown eyes showing his offence.

"Babe, are you going to just let him talk to me like that?"

"She said she wants you to leave."

The three of us turn to look at Brax. Josh's mouth falls open as he tries to regain his composure.

"I don't know why you two are even getting involved. You're not her family."

That comment hurts more than it should. I step forward, slapping Josh across the face much to the surprise of everyone, including myself.

"They mean more to me than you ever will, Joshua. We're done. Get that through your thick skull. I want nothing to do with you. There will never be an 'us' again. Just fucking leave me alone."

Silence fills our little circle. Mrs. Griffin next door walks out her front door in her dressing gown, giving us a small wave. I awkwardly wave back, before walking around Josh to head inside.

Mom and Dad's cars aren't in the driveway, and I'm thankful that I can escape to my room without question. I hear footsteps come inside a few seconds after and I turn to make sure it's just the three guys, and not Captain Fuckwit following.

Tyler, Brax and Nate stand at the front door watching me. I give in, looking at Brax and Nate, my heart pulling at their concerned faces. I quickly focus back on Tyler, giving him a small smile. He's an asshole, but he's my brother, and he has my back when it's most important. He returns my gesture with a nod before heading to the living room.

Turning away, I climb the stairs to my room, feeling two sets of eyes on my retreating back. I should talk to them about last night and get the answers I desperately crave.

But not right now.

Right now, I need to do the only thing that helps distract me.

I need to watch the goriest horror movie I can find.

# Chapter 10

"**A**udie, I'm worried about you," Mom says from across the table.

I look up, midway through picking apart my lunch. "Huh? Why?"

Mom delicately places her fork down and folds her hands together.

"You've been so quiet since your trip. Did something happen? Did you and Tyler fight again?"

It's been three days since coming back from Salem. I've spent most of that time in my room, buried in cliterature as I try not to think about the witch hunt. Joshua has thankfully left me alone, though it appears our confrontation did the trick as he just updated his Facebook status this morning to say he's in a new relationship with Carly. I promptly unfriended him, and have made every effort to stay off socials for the next few days.

I give Mom a reassuring smile. "No, just tired I think. It's been a weird few days."

She nods, understanding. "Don't worry about Joshua. Boys will come and go, Audie. You're still young and deserve much better than that."

"I know," I say earnestly. "Don't stress. He's not on my mind now."

Tyler lets out a groan as he walks into the kitchen. He's in exercise gear and sweating.

"Seven miles. Man, I am beat. It's freezing outside."

I shake my head, pushing my plate away. "Personally, I can't wait for the snow to start. Hot coffees and books by the fireplace."

"Nerd," Tyler whispers, earning a playful shove from Mom as he walks past.

Mom rolls her eyes, looking between the two of us. "You pair... Gosh, never a dull moment in this house."

"He started it," I say, laughing as Tyler gives me the finger behind Mom's back.

"So, what's the plans for today?" Mom asks.

Tyler sits down next to me, picking up an apple from the fruit bowl on the table. "Brax and Nate are swinging by at some point to play video games. Other than that, sweet fuck all."

"Tyler!" Mom scolds.

"Sorry," he mumbles, through a mouth full of apple.

I swallow hard, staring down at my plate. Brax and Nate coming over is going to cause some difficulties. It looks like another day of hiding out in my bedroom.

Mom grabs our plates and takes them to the sink. "I have to pop out to the shops, but I'll be back soon. Dad will also be home late tonight, so we're going to order pizza for dinner."

"Sounds good," I reply, pushing my chair back. "I'll be in my room if you need me."

***

I'm halfway through Mine by A.K. Rose, when my phone dings. I put my book down, clicking open the screen to read a text message from Mom asking if I need anything from the shops. I send back a short reply before going back to my inbox.

My heart halts as I spot an unread message from Halloween. It's from Nate, and judging by the timestamp, it was sent just after we got back to the inn from the witch hunt.

*Nate: You're absolutely perfect. We can't believe you gave us the honor of being your first. Let's talk soon.*

I re-read the message a few times, shocked that I missed it. They must think I'm the biggest bitch, and that I'm ignoring them. Too many days have passed to send a message back now, so perhaps it's better this way.

Sighing, I put my phone down and go back to reading. I can no longer concentrate, my eyes glazing over the words without absorbing them.

A knock on my bedroom door makes me jump, and I look over, waiting for Tyler to appear. When it remains closed, I put the book down and move to get up.

"Just come in already."

The door slowly opens, and I'm left speechless as I spot Brax and Nate in the hallway.

"What are you doing here?" I manage to choke out, trying to act normal.

They step inside, closing the door behind them. Brax gives me a small smile as he leans against the wall, placing a bag at his feet.

"We just wanted to check in on you. We haven't heard from you."

I look at the door hesitantly. "Where's Tyler?"

Nate laughs. "Idiot thinks he dropped his phone during his run. He's out looking for it. He'll be quite awhile."

I frown, which quickly changes to a look of confusion as Brax pulls out Tyler's phone from his pocket. "He'll be gone for a bit. We just needed some privacy."

"You stole his phone?" I ask in disbelief.

Brax shrugs. "Borrowed temporarily. We need to talk."

"What about?" I respond quickly, looking away.

Nate approaches the bed to stand in front of me. "You're avoiding us. You haven't texted me back, and you have hidden in your room every time we've come over. Come on, Audrey, let's talk about it."

"I don't know what to say," I admit honestly. "It was fun. And amazing. But what more can I say or do? I don't know where to go from here."

Brax sits on the end of the bed, watching me carefully. "We get that. I can understand how confusing shit must be right now. But we've spoken about things and we don't want it to just be a one-off."

I look between the two of them with confusion. "What do you mean?"

Nate reaches out, grabbing my hand. "We want to take you on a date. What do you say?"

"A date?" I repeat. "Like a date-date? The three of us?"

They laugh lightly. "Well, maybe not a triangle situation straight away. We would take you on dates separately. But we want to give it a shot," Brax says.

I shake my head as I process their words. "You want me to date you both? Can you imagine Tyler's reaction? Gosh, what about my parents? Or yours?"

"What about them? It's our business and we can work it out as we go along. We don't need to make rules or work out logistics yet," Nate replies.

"I can't. It will fuck up your friendship with Tyler if things go south."

Brax snorts. "No, it won't. We've been friends for too long. We can handle him. But we just want you. Maybe it won't work out, or maybe it will. But, we won't know unless we try."

I glance between the two of them. I know logically I should say no, but for once, I just want to do what my heart wants.

"I guess I could go on a date with you," I murmur. "But if things start going downhill, we need to stop and be platonic. You guys mean too much to me to fuck up our friendship. And Tyler, he'd never forgive me if I came between you."

Nate gently pushes me back onto the bed, leaning over me with his hands on either side of my head. "Oh, babe. Don't you worry. The only way you'll be coming between us is when we're all naked and making you scream our names."

He leans down, crashing his lips against mine. A moan gets caught in my throat as I kiss him back, my hands gripping his solid biceps. I feel hands grab my bare feet, pushing them apart. I try to catch a glimpse of Brax, but Nate stops me.

"It's my turn to taste you."

He reaches down, grabbing my shirt and pulling it off my body. His hands immediately go for my breasts, squeezing them through my lacy bra.

Brax unbuttons my pants, pulling them down my legs with my underwear. I lift my hips to assist, pushing into Nate. I'm pulled forward off the bed, Nate reaching behind me to unclasp my bra before he lowers me back down.

I look between them. "Well, this isn't fair. I'm naked and you're not."

Nate's hand swings out to grab my throat. "We know. But we're in charge, not you."

I gasp, tilting my head back as I lock eyes with Nate. Behind him, Brax grabs my ankles and I feel familiar texture. I sneak a peek, spotting the infamous red rope in his hand.

Brax weaves it around my ankle, before doing the same to the other one. He spreads my legs apart, exposing me as he ties the rope to my bedframe.

Automatically, I try to move my legs, but they are held down tight to the bed. I can't move them, and before I know it, my hands are bound together with duct tape.

"Such a pretty girl," Brax says, standing back to admire his work. "I'd love to have you like this all day. God, I can see your pussy getting wet already."

I throw my head back, a whimper escaping through my lips as I submit to their control. Nate moves between my legs, his mouth trailing hot kisses up my inner thigh.

"Our perfect girl. I bet you taste just as good too."

His tongue swipes out, licking my pussy. I pant, my body springing to life, as he swirls his tongue around my clit.

Brax's thumb strokes my bottom lip. "Open your mouth."

I obey, and he slips his index and middle fingers in. "Suck on them," he says, watching me through heated eyes. I close my mouth around his digits, sucking them until he tells me to stop.

I watch as he moves away, just in time for Nate to pull away from my sex. Holding up his wet fingers to show me, he leans over, lowering them down and pushing them into my pussy.

My body throbs as he fucks me with his fingers, his eyes on my face as he watches my expression.

"This pussy belongs to us," he says, his spare hand pulling off his shirt and unbuttoning his jeans. "And one day soon, your ass too."

My eyes widen at his words, but I don't have time to react as he positions himself between my legs, and thrusts into my body. I cry out blissfully, welcoming the sweet feeling. His hands grab my hips, digging in hard enough to leave bruises. Brax starts thrusting hard and fast, pulling me down and impaling me on his cock.

Nate strips his clothes off, stroking his length as he grabs my hair with his free hand. "Open," he says briskly.

My lips barely part before the tip of his cock pushes into my warm mouth. My head turns to the side, trying to find a comfortable angle as he slowly starts fucking my mouth.

His grip doesn't ease up on my hair, his fist pulling my head towards him as he meets me half way with his hips.

"Fuck, you're a good girl. You going to come on Brax's cock?"

I moan, trying to nod as best as I can, but it's difficult. I'm being pounded from both ends, my legs tied down, restricting my movement.

Brax's fingers find my clit, his hand rubbing against it. My body responds, tightening around him as I feel the pressure build.

"Do you want to come?" asks Brax, his relenting thrusts going deep.

I mumble confirmation against Nate's hard cock, my eyes rolling back as I start to crash.

"Then come for me," he says, pinching my clit.

My body explodes, my orgasm ripping through me. My bound hands claw at Nate's lower abdomen, trying to ground myself as I ride the waves. They both continue fucking me, their pace brutal, and I realize I've closed my eyes. My body relaxes and sags as my climax ends, my heart racing like a freight train.

Suddenly, Brax pulls out of me, followed a few seconds later by Nate. My eyes flutter open, watching as they stroke themselves fast. Brax lets out a low groan, his release spilling onto my stomach. Nate reaches down, grabbing my throat as he stops moving the hand on his cock. His own orgasm hits him, his release decorating me along with Brax's.

I look up at them in revelation, a little moan escaping, as Nate kisses me, his hand still locked on my throat.

"There," he mutters, pulling back slightly. "Now, we've marked you. You're ours."

Brax hums in agreement, his hand caressing my thigh. "Ours."

Nate releases my throat, his finger tracing over the cut on my chest. "Our pretty little ruined Red."

"I'm not ruined yet," I try to argue, giving them a smile.

"We'll see about that," Brax says, untying my legs and pulling the duct tape off my wrists.

Nate leans down, scooping me up in his arms, and carrying me towards my bathroom door. "I guess we'll just have to hunt you down again."

"You can try," I say, wrapping my arms around his neck. "But you have to catch me first."

They both chuckle and Nate stops, lowering me until my feet touch the floor. He turns, picking up the discarded bag on the ground. Brax grabs a fistful of my hair and pulls my head back to look at him. I watch as Nate hands something over to him, and I suck in a breath at the sight of the neon masks. They slowly put their masks on, the orange and blue lights flashing to life. Brax lets go of my hair, taking a step back.

"Then what are you waiting for? Start running, witch."

www.ingramcontent.com/pod-product-compliance
Lightning Source LLC
Chambersburg PA
CBHW070412200726
48294CB00003B/1178